Elvi
Ron

and

Fiesta de Santa Fe featuring
Zozobra's Great Escape

by Andrew Leo Lovato

Museum of New Mexico Press, Santa Fe

Dedication

For my mother and father, Priscilla and Joe Lovato; you embody the true spirit of Santa Fe.

Special thanks to Fran Levine of the New Mexico History Museum and Erica Garcia of the National Hispanic Cultural Center for your support and ideas; Anna Gallegos and Mary Wachs at the Museum of New Mexico Press for your efforts in making this project a reality.

Contents

S IMPORTANT as the Fiesta de Santa Fe is to adults in the community, children are the lifeblood of our annual celebration. Chasing candy thrown from floats at the Historical/Hysterical Parade, walking beside costumed animals at the Pet Parade, solemnly attending the novenas and Fiesta masses, children have made the Fiesta the inimitable event that it is.

As I travel back through the ethers of time, I land as a ten-year-old boy in 1964 in a much different Santa Fe than exists today. The population of the city was about thirty-five thousand souls, less than half its current number. What is now considered the south side of Santa Fe—everything south of the intersection of Cerrillos Road and St. Michaels Drive—seemed like an undeveloped wilderness of arroyos, cholla plants, and blue-bellied lizards.

Things that happened in the bigger world were reconfigured through the filter of the Sangre de Cristo Mountains to arrive in Santa Fe in a simpler, more abstract form, transformed by the bright sunshine and the high mountain air and then mixed with traditional Hispanic culture to create a fantasyland of influences. We absorbed yo-yos, hula hoops, and the Beatles seamlessly into our world of mariachi music, La Llorona, and piñon picking.

Santa Fe was our playground, and my childhood was pretty typical for a Santa Fe muchacho. Aside from going to school, we spent most of our time riding bikes with high handlebars and banana seats around the narrow winding streets, exploring the back alleys and the nooks and crannies of the city until the sun went down.

Our parents weren't particularly fearful of any harm coming to us when we were out roaming on our own. There was a general trust among the adults that the children were being looked after by everyone in the community. Santa Fe was a safe place to grow up, and bad things happened only in places far away.

The Santa Fe Fiesta is an especially vivid memory for me. If I close my eyes, I can still hear the St. Francis Cathedral bells tolling and can recall the smell of Indian tacos, burritos, and carne adovada wafting from the food booths that lined the Plaza.

The Fiesta holds vivid impressions for those who grew up in Santa Fe or visited from northern New Mexico's smaller villages in the 1960s to experience the sights, sounds, and smells of the city's biggest party. The Plaza was bedecked in its finest decorations, with brightly painted coats of arms (*escudos*) of the founding families that accompanied Vargas in the reconquest of Santa Fe. Wooden paintings of saints (*retablos*) generously adorned the Plaza, hanging from trees and portals. It is not so difficult if I close my eyes to see the dazzling Fiesta Queen, newly crowned by the archbishop of Santa Fe, gracing the Plaza with her royal court. The gallant Caballeros awe-inspiring in their colorful gold capes, red sashes, plumed hats, and shiny black boots, atop majestic horses.

The Fiesta celebrations of the 1960s had a carnival air, punctuated by the mass of humanity that circled endlessly around the

Plaza. It seemed like everyone knew each other. Often the boys would walk one way around the Plaza, while the girls would circle in the opposite direction. The first pass would be acknowledged with a smile, the second with a wink. The third would end with hand-holding and a mutual direction.

The Fiesta was filled with balloons and toy vendors on every corner, and cotton candy in all colors of the rainbow to tempt the youngsters. Children hounded their parents for coins for the Fiesta rides. The favorite was Tio Vivo, a colorful wooden merry-go-round with beautifully painted horses, hand cranked by assorted young men who wanted to make a few extra dollars. Some lucky children mounted real live burros that were liveried on Burro Alley and were treated to a ride around the Plaza.

Santa Fe children always made sure to attend La Merienda de la Fiesta, a historical fashion show with afternoon refreshments. It featured traditional Spanish fashions modeled by Merienda members. The young Fiesta-goers were not as interested in heirloom fashions as they were in sipping the complimentary rich Spanish chocolate and sampling the sweet biscochitos that melted in your mouth.

The music and dancing on the Plaza went on continuously for three days, beginning on Friday after the burning of Zozobra. The Baile de Gente began the nonstop public street dancing. On the Plaza bandstand, elaborately costumed local girls enthusiastically displayed what they had learned in Spanish dance classes, mariachi bands from Old Mexico played *rancheras*, and local bands (*los musicos*) supplied a steady mix of rock and Spanish music, making sure to play their own obligatory versions of "La Bamba."

The children of Santa Fe were free to wander the streets during the celebration while their parents occupied themselves with the De Vargas Ball at La Fonda Hotel and the Fiesta Melodrama presented by the Santa Fe Community Theatre, which poked fun at everyone and everything, including local politicians and national figures.

The Fiesta parades held a special fascination for the children of Santa Fe. On Saturday morning, the Desfile de los Niños

(Children's Pet Parade) featured children marching through the streets with their dogs, cats, horses, monkeys, rabbits, and other assorted creatures. The animals and their owners strutted by decked out in a variety of hats, dresses, and extravagant costumes.

The Desfile de la Gente (Historical/Hysterical Parade) on Sunday afternoon was a dizzying spectacle of horses and *caballeros*, floats, low-rider cars, high school marching bands, politicians, and the ever-present Quisicosas (Anything Goes) Clowns.

The cleanup crew following the parade consisted of a legendary character by the name of Shorty. He cleaned up behind the horses with a broom, dustpan, and bucket. He was compensated for his services after the parade, when everyone bought him a drink at the Plaza Bar.

The Fiesta appropriately came to an end with the solemn walk to the Cross of the Martyrs, brilliantly illuminated by floodlights in the fading dusk. Bonfires marked the path that people climbed in a procession culminating at the top of the hill for the evening commemoration service. The Montezuma Choir, from a seminary for Mexican priests in Las Vegas, chanted hymns. After the ceremony, good-byes were said, and another Santa Fe Fiesta was history. Exhausted parents searched for kids, and families eventually made their way back home, tired but happy.

The pageantry and color of the Fiesta de Santa Fe is etched in the memories of the generations of children who have experienced it. One event likely stands out as the most memorable of all: the burning of Zozobra.

Santa Feans may remember driving to Fort Marcy Field in the mid-1960s, when admission was $3 per car, having picnics on the grass, and listening to the mariachis play. They may also recall the mesmerizing scene of the Quetzalcoatl Dancers, the white-robed Glooms, and finally the Fire Dancer, wearing red, white, and blue streamers, taunting Zozobra before lighting the fuse that set him on fire to yells of "Burn, burn, burn!" Poor Old Man Gloom protested in an agonized voice as he was quickly engulfed in a torrent of flames and crumbled in ashes as fireworks lit up the sky behind him. This sensational and enigmatic ritual indicated that another Fiesta was under way.

THE FOLLOWING STORY DEPICTS the adventures of Elvis Romero and his best friend and cousin, Pepa. It is a view of the Fiesta and Santa Fe culture through the eyes of children in the 1960s. It can be characterized as a story about children, but it is not just for children. I envision this tale being read by grandparents to their grandchildren, with all enjoying it equally as memories of Fiestas past are revived. It addresses the universal themes of justice, right triumphing over wrong, and the struggle to be moral in a complex world.

My inspiration for this story comes from a question: If Huck Finn had grown up in Santa Fe in the 1960s, rather than on the Mississippi River in the mid-1800s, would he have acted similarly to Elvis and Pepa and faced similar philosophical quandaries?

I ask for your indulgence with the fantastical nature of this tale as I invoke the tradition of magical realism. People often comment that Santa Fe was an enchanting place to live in the 1960s. This is an attempt to capture the flavor that made the city so special for locals and visitors alike.

THE CHILDREN'S PARADE, ca. 1940s. New Mexico Magazine Collection, courtesy Palace of the Governors Photo Archives (NMHM/DCA).

Left
ELEGANTLY COSTUMED SPANISH DANCERS, ca. 1940s-1950s, add color and style to the Fiesta de Santa Fe. Traditional New Mexican dances, such as polkas, waltzes, and rancheras, were among the cultural offerings of Fiesta. New Mexico Magazine Collection, courtesy Palace of the Governors Photo Archives (NMHM/DCA).

THE DESFILE DE LOS NIÑOS,
or Children's Parade, in 1938. The
parade is long a perennial favorite for
Fiesta goers. Traditionally presented
on Saturday morning during Fiesta
weekend, elaborately costumed
children and their pets take center
stage. Photo by Harold Humes, courtesy Palace of the Governors Photo
Archives (NMHM/DCA), 150443.

**ZOZOBRA UNDER CON-
STRUCTION**, 1959. Photo by Steve
Northrup, courtesy Palace of the
Governors Photo Archives (NMHM/
DCA), 10909.

Zozob
Great

ra's
Escape

I WISH TO WELCOME ALL MY READERS, young and old, and beg your indulgence as I recount an adventure of some forty years ago, when my cousin Pepa and I were ten-year-olds. The Santa Fe of 1964 that I look back on was quite a different place from what it is today. In those days, there were half as many people, and life moved at a slower pace. Everything that happened in the larger world passed through the filter of the Sangre de Cristo Mountains and arrived in Santa Fe in a simpler, more tranquil form, touched by the bright sunshine and the high mountain air.

Pepa and I loved growing up in Santa Fe, and we spent most of our days riding our bikes all over town. Like many of the kids we knew, our favorite time of the year was the Fiesta de Santa Fe. The sights, sounds, and smells overwhelmed our senses and filled our hearts with joy.

Here is my recollection of one particular Fiesta that will always be unforgettable for me and I'm sure for Pepa as well. This is our story, as best as I am able to put into words, of the year we tried to change the course of Fiesta forever.

FOR GENERATIONS, Santa Fe children have been captivated by the image of Zozobra. Replicas of Will Shuster's creation have commonly sprung up in backyards and have been the focus of school projects during Fiesta season. This elaborate likeness was made in 1955. Photo courtesy Palace of the Governors Photo Archives (NMHM/DCA), 136981.

T WAS EARLY SEPTEMBER, and the last glorious days of summer had finally come to an end. As I began to stir uneasily from a deep, dark sleep, I let out a groan. I buried my head under my pillow in a vain attempt to ward off the blinding rays of the morning sun. It seemed so unfair to be given a taste of the good life during summer vacation, only to be yanked back into the harsh reality of schoolbooks and stern nuns.

I yawned forlornly, half-dozing in an unfinished dream, waiting for my mom to call me. My body felt as if it were made out of adobe bricks, thick and heavy.

"How will I ever be able to get up and move?" I thought. "Maybe I'm sick with that flu that's going around."

Slowly, like a bubble rising from the bottom of a deep pond, a realization came over me; a magical healing power transformed my entire being: It was Saturday! I suddenly felt a surge of life flowing through my arms and legs, like the rejuvenated limbs of a dry cholla cactus after a desert thunderstorm. I jumped up from my bed and was out the front door and on my bike with the speed of a roadrunner in full stride.

As I pedaled down a bumpy dirt road, I felt the cool morning air wash over my face. My hair sailed over my forehead as I raced toward my cousin Pepa's house. When I reached the front yard of the large adobe casa, I stepped hard on my brakes and spun around in a circle, raising a large cloud of dust to signal my arrival.

My Tia Sophia looked out from behind her kitchen window and waved her hand, white with tortilla flour. I liked my tia; she always seemed happy to see me and had a jar full of biscochitos to prove it.

"How is your family, *mijito*?"

"Everyone is fine, Tia. Is Pepa awake yet?"

"*Mi Dios!* My poor Francesca is dead to the world, Elvis. Last time I checked, she looked like a sack of pinto beans lying on her bed."

We both laughed. My tia always called Pepa by her formal name, but everybody else just called her Pepa.

Before I go on with the story, there is something that I should probably clarify. That is, while we're on the subject of names, it seems like the first question anyone ever asks me is if I was named after the king of rock 'n' roll. I can't tell you how many times I've had to explain that my mother was a bit of a rebel for her time. Rather than picking out a nice, traditional Catholic name like Miguel or Marcos, she'd opted for Elvis after she saw the thick shock of black hair that I came into the world with. Now that that's settled, my dear tia announced to me.

"It's time Francesca got up and went outside for some fresh air. Come into the kitchen, Elvis, and have a couple of biscochitos while I wake that sleepy head."

As I licked the last crumbs from my hands, Pepa rushed into the kitchen and said, "Let's go!"

Out the door we went, but not before we'd reached into the biscochito jar and stuffed our pockets for the road. We jumped on our bikes with a flair that would have made Zorro proud. Off we went, blazing our way toward destinations unknown.

"Pepa, what do you want to do?"

"I don't know. What you want to do?"

It didn't seem to matter that this was the same introduction we used every time we got together. It always seemed full of promise spoken on a new day.

I was almost a head shorter than Pepa, although we were both ten years old. Pepa had two long brown ponytails that hung down her back. Her most distinguishing feature was her luminous green eyes. She always wore the same faded blue jeans, black Converse tennis shoes, and her beloved LA Dodgers baseball cap. Pepa definitely dressed for comfort rather than style.

Not only were we cousins, but we had been best friends since Pepa and her family had moved from Española into my neighborhood. Some kids at school gave me a hard time because my best friend was a girl, but I didn't listen to them and neither did Pepa. All we knew was that there was nobody else in the world that we had more fun hanging out with.

We rode in silence for a while, weaving our way through the little dirt roads that led to the Plaza. As we neared the center of town, I saw women in long, colorful skirts wearing silver and turquoise jewelry, carrying pots of posole, and calling after children who shrieked and played in the redbrick streets. Men stood in tight circles smoking hand-rolled cigarettes and laughing loudly.

There was no mistaking it, Fiesta was in the air. People could put down their everyday burdens and celebrate for a few short days with mariachi music, good food, and dancing on the Plaza.

We were particularly ready to begin our celebration during the autumn of 1964. It had not been an easy year for our small New Mexico town. The skies had remained crystal blue and bone dry almost the entire summer. Once in a while, fluffy dark clouds passed over the fiery sun and brought a few seconds of relief to the panting dogs that lay under the porches of the adobe homes. But the clouds never stayed for long or amounted to much. Instead they continued on their way to other, more fortunate places, where life-giving rain fell.

The acequias that normally flowed with dark brown water were cracked and filled with sand. No water ran down from the high mountains to fill them so they could, in turn, feed the thirsty fields of the farmers. The bean, corn, and chili plants drooped their shoulders under the oppressive sun, which never seemed to grow tired or take even a momentary siesta during that eternal summer. It was no wonder that we were ready to forget our troubles for a little while and indulge in the upcoming Fiesta celebrations.

Pepa and I sat under the portal in front of the Palace of the Governors and watched the activities. A group of men were hard at work on a wooden stage for the Fiesta entertainment, scheduled to begin on Friday evening. We watched their swinging hammers gleam in the sun.

After a few minutes, we became restless and decided to hop back on our bikes and ride up Washington Avenue, which led north from the Plaza toward Fort Marcy Park.

As we neared the park, we beheld an unbelievable spectacle. Suddenly, on this beautiful day that had seemed so full of promise, I was filled with foreboding. A huge orange-haired puppet, with saucer eyes radiating fear and sorrow, was spread across the infield of the ballpark.

By the third base dugout, a group of men were busy constructing a frame of two-by-four studs for the giant, sad-eyed figure. We sat upright on our bikes, riveted by the sight.

Pepa and I were familiar with this melancholy giant, who was called Zozobra, but we had never seen him up close before.

Every year a new Zozobra was created and then burned in a ritual that signified the beginning of the Fiesta. Zozobra symbolized gloom, sorrow, and bad luck. He was the embodiment of terror and evil, the dark side of life, the stuff of nightmares. Zozobra was created for only one purpose: to die. His death in flames symbolized the triumph of good over evil. Zozobra's death meant new life for everyone celebrating the Santa Fe Fiesta. The merriment could begin with a sense of new beginnings.

A flood of remorse filled me as I witnessed the sacrificial preparations taking place in front of us. Feelings of impending doom and anxiety washed over me as I stared, transfixed. Pepa's eyes welled up with tears as she viewed the helpless, bewildered giant being prepared for his horrible destiny.

"How can they do this to him? He hasn't done anything to hurt anybody!" I cried.

Pepa replied, "My mama told me last Fiesta that he was burning to get rid of all the bad things and bad luck that had happened all year, so that we could start brand new and have more fun during Fiesta."

"Well, I don't think it's fair. It's not his fault that the sky doesn't rain."

"Yeah, that's true," Pepa agreed. "Like my uncle said, it was bad luck when the motor in his truck broke down a couple of months ago, and it turned out that he forgot to put oil in it. You can't blame that on Zozobra."

"Yeah, remember when the pipes busted at the school last winter when it was real cold? We got to miss a whole week of school. It might have been bad luck for the nuns, but it was good luck for us."

"Yeah, you're right, Elvis," laughed Pepa. "I wish someone would come and rescue Zozobra."

At that moment, our eyes met with a mutual understanding of entwined destiny. We both knew that a higher mission was being bestowed upon us and a larger plan was responsible for the actions that were about to take place. We felt a shiver of fear mixed with euphoria as we sealed our resolve with a secret oath to somehow right the terrible injustice that was being perpetrated on this innocent victim.

We did not undertake our budding mission lightly. We were both good kids who tried to obey our parents and always do the right thing. We realized that we were treading on dangerous ground and that many people might not share our convictions. Despite our heavy yoke of apprehension, we felt compelled to fight this impending crime.

Reluctantly, we rode back down Washington Avenue toward the Woolworth's store on the Plaza. Woolworth's was the largest five-and-dime in Santa Fe. It was filled with a mind-boggling variety of merchandise. People could find everything from shoes and winter clothes to goldfish or the latest 45 records played on the local radio station, KVSF. Pretty Priscilla, as she was known to the locals, was always behind the counter, ready to assist you with a smile.

We were drawn to the generous selection of sweet candies the store had displayed in large glass jars. We could buy two candies for a penny. With the modest sum of five cents, quite a horde could be acquired. Feasting on gum balls and licorice sticks, we devised our history-altering plan.

The first problem we chewed over was the physical dilemma of moving such a large victim out of danger. Even if we could do this, what would we do with him? Where would we hide him? What would happen if we got caught? Pepa and I pondered over these weighty issues, our jaws working feverishly on gum balls as we sat on a park bench. We also needed to devise and implement a plan quickly. In a few days, Zozobra's funeral pyre would be completed, and he would be impaled on the structure, making it impossible to carry out a rescue.

The grave situation provided us with the necessary inspiration for an ingenious design to rescue Zozobra. We decided to meet late the following night in the bean and squash fields of Victor Gonzales, Pepa's uncle.

To put an end to her constant badgering, that summer Victor had taught Pepa how to drive an ancient three-gear tractor that he used to plow the fields. It had been a good summer to train her. Without rain, Victor's fields were mostly barren, so there was little danger of Pepa running over any valuable crops.

That rusty old tractor was perfect for dragging Zozobra to safety, and Pepa knew that her uncle kept a spare key for it under a black rock in front of his tool shed. Because the tractor was parked far from Victor's house, he wouldn't hear us start it up or realize that it was missing. All we needed were a few ropes to hitch Zozobra up to the back of the contraption. We'd secure them from Victor's tool shed without anyone being the wiser.

We decided that the best place to stow Zozobra away was up the road, east of Fort Marcy Park. The road led to Hyde Park and the Santa Fe National Forest. It was a mountainous recreation area, mostly uninhabited. Numerous wooded spots not far up the road would be perfect for hiding a large, orange-haired puppet. We figured we could carry out the entire task in less than two hours, return the tractor, and be back in bed before anyone knew we were gone. We laid out the final details of the plan and made a pact to carry out the monumental feat. We returned to our respective homes that afternoon with our hearts fortified and our wills set. Tomorrow night we would turn the course of destiny on its ear and strike a blow for justice. Zozobra would not burn!

The next day was uneventful. Pepa and I stayed close to home and went over the coming night in our heads. We did not even feel compelled to see each other one last time before our rendezvous.

My mother was a little concerned about my health and asked if I was feeling well. It was very unusual to have me around the house on a warm fall day. My pale, worried look also led her to suspect that I was a little under the weather. I insisted that I was fine and just felt like hanging around the house. As I waited in my bedroom for the minutes and hours to pass, I refined our plot a little more.

Dragging Zozobra up Artist Road, with its rocks and rough pavement, would probably damage the giant puppet. So I found a large laundry bag filled with old blankets that my mother intended to donate to the Salvation Army. I hid the bag in the alley behind our house. If we wrapped Zozobra in the blankets before we began pulling him, he'd be protected from the jagged terrain we'd be navigating that evening. I also gathered a smaller bag of supplies, including a flashlight, a pocket knife, and a bag of potato chips.

My mom, using her keen powers of maternal observation, noticed my strange behavior during the late afternoon and early evening. I usually ate as if I had been fasting with the Penitentes, but I only picked at my food during supper, even though she had cooked green chili, beans, and tamales that afternoon. Equally unusual was my desire to go to bed early. My mom could not remember the last time she did not have to prod, threaten, and plead to get me into bed. She put her hand on my forehead and tucked me in. She felt no sign of fever and sighed. She concluded that her little boy was probably just worn out from school and the mountain of homework the nuns gave him.

I listened to my mom washing the supper dishes as my dad sat in the living room reading the newspaper. After what seemed like an eternity, the dishes were done, and my dad turned off the lights in the house. My parents retired to their bedroom, speaking in low voices for a few minutes. Finally everything was still, and the house was quiet. My younger brother, Angelo, was spending the night at his friend's house. This made my task infinitely easier.

I slowly slid out of bed and pulled my clothes on. I discreetly stepped out the back door and bounded across the backyard. I hoisted my waiting bags of supplies onto the handlebars of my bike and was soon riding down the dark, sleepy streets toward Zozobra and my waiting accomplice.

I looked up and saw glittering stars that I hadn't noticed before. I'd never been down these streets after dark. They were transformed, like strange streets in another town. Some of the houses I passed were dark and silent. Others were illuminated by the flickering blue light of TV sets. A few dogs barked accusingly as I glided past, as if to tell me that I should be home in bed at this hour. At last I reached the top of Washington Avenue, continued up Bishop's Lodge Road, and came upon Fort Marcy Park.

I gazed over the deserted baseball diamond, which was dimly lit by a half-moon rising over the mountains. A streak of anxiety ran through me as I saw the large sleeping figure lying in wait for his rescue.

I thought to myself, "Was this really such a good idea after all?" Perhaps it would be better if we forgot this whole crazy scheme and went home. Somehow everything seemed easier in the daylight.

The pale moonlight reflecting off the pasty white complexion of Zozobra's bewildered face created an eerie picture that troubled me. I closed my eyes and remembered my oath to Pepa the day before. This was no time to back out. How would I ever be able to face her if I abandoned poor, helpless Zozobra now? I hopped on my bike and continued on toward Victor's fields and my waiting comrade.

As I neared, I could see Pepa's silhouette perched on the tractor, gazing toward Fort Marcy, as if she were also exorcising her last demons before our moment of truth. I interrupted Pepa's contemplation with a short whistle. She twirled around quickly with a nervous expression, which eased when she recognized me.

"Hey, Elvis," whispered Pepa. "What's in the bags?"

"Stuff we'll need for rescuing Zozobra."

Pepa jumped off the tractor and began rummaging around in a woodshed, gathering more supplies. I held a flashlight and shined the light on different areas. Pepa gathered up all the rope she could find. She stuffed it into one of the bags, and we hoisted them onto the tractor.

"I guess that's it," said Pepa. "I hope Victor doesn't hear us when we start it up."

She made the sign of the cross by touching her forehead, the middle of her chest, then her left and right shoulders with the middle finger of her right hand. She pulled a rusty key out of her pocket and slipped it into the ignition of the old machine with the peeling red paint. She turned the key, and the stillness of the night was broken by the sputtering sound of the tractor's complaining engine. Pepa began pumping the gas pedal with her right foot. The engine wheezed and rumbled, coming to life as a puff of black smoke escaped from the exhaust pipe.

The tractor was a hundred times louder than we remembered. We were afraid it would wake not only Victor but the whole town.

I climbed behind the single tractor seat Pepa occupied and sat on a fender. Pepa nervously pulled the stick shift into gear, and the tractor lurched forward across the dark fields.

My anxiety subsided as we crossed the bumpy terrain. When we reached a wooden gate at the south end of the property, Pepa shifted into neutral and jumped down to open it. I secured the gate to an old post with a loose piece of baling wire.

She let out a long sigh and exclaimed, "Here we go!"

If any casual observers had been around, it would have been a strange sight indeed: a ten-year-old girl and boy meandering down Paseo de Peralta in the middle of the night, sitting stiffly on an ancient, puffing tractor. The moon rose a little higher in the sky. Several suspicious dogs began to bark at the apparitions invading their territory.

After what seemed like an eternity, we reached Fort Marcy Park. Pepa guided the steering wheel to the right. We rolled onto the thick, green grass of the outfield. Due to a recently installed sprinkler system, the baseball field sported lush grass, even though the rest of the town wilted under the drought. While the modern sprinkler system was a great source of pride to city leaders, it was a hindrance to Pepa. She wove around the jutting metal booby traps that could have taken out a tractor tire with just one false move.

At long last, we reached the feet of the martyr, who lay ashen faced and quiet in the pale moonlight. The silent sufferer was such a pitiful sight that I felt my resolve returning and summoned my courage.

Gingerly, Pepa turned the key, and the sputtering engine came to a stop. We jumped down and stood gazing at Zozobra. Up close, Zozobra looked different than the image we had constructed in our minds. He was much larger and more crudely pieced together than the animated figure we remembered. Still, this impressive creation of lumber, wire, and paper captured our sympathy.

I felt a chill run down my back and I shivered slightly.

"Zozobra sure is huge! Do you really think we can move him?"

Pepa shrugged her shoulders and laughed nervously.

She turned to the tractor and pulled down the bag containing the blankets and rope. In a matter-of-fact voice, she said, "Well, I guess it's time for us to get to work."

Without another word, we began sliding ropes under Zozobra at strategic points of his anatomy. One rope was tied to his black-belted waist and then around the frame of the tractor. We also tied ropes to Zozobra's shoulders and neck and attached them to the hitch. We bound his muslin-covered arms tightly around his body, so they would not be damaged. We cradled his large hands in blankets and rested them on his stomach as he lay on his back.

We worked quickly and intently. Time seemed to stand still in the dark ballpark as sweat beads formed on our foreheads. The large wooden legs, constructed of chicken wire and white cloth, needed to be wrapped in blankets and tied together tightly to ease Zozobra's journey. Finally, we covered Zozobra's head with a thick blanket and secured it slightly off the ground.

Although the entire process took about thirty minutes, it felt like an eternity. It seemed like the eyes of the entire city were peering down on us. We wasted a little time after the last rope was tied, admiring our handiwork.

"Let's go," commanded Pepa, as she climbed on the tractor and started it up. I scrambled back onto the fender with my heart racing. Pepa shoved the tractor into gear, and slowly we began to move along the grass with our precious cargo in tow.

As I surveyed the scene, I realized that it was not possible to leave the park the same way we had entered. The sprinklers jutting out of the grass posed too great a threat. If Zozobra got caught on one of the sprinkler extensions, it would tear him apart. There was only one way to exit. We had to turn behind the third base dugout and follow a small emergency road that crossed an old wooden bridge.

We carefully maneuvered the turn and headed toward the exit road. I kept an eagle eye on Zozobra as we went along, to make sure he didn't get bumped around too much. The old blankets kept him from being ripped apart by the rocks and dirt.

We chugged along until we reached the wooden bridge, which crossed an arroyo.

As we approached the bridge, Pepa turned to me and said, "Jump down and guide his legs so they don't fall off the side." I dragged Zozobra's legs to line up with the crossing.

When I turned to return to the tractor, I caught sight of something that made my heart start beating like a drum at an Indian dance. It was the figure of a man crawling up from under the bridge in the dim light. I stood frozen as he stumbled out of the arroyo toward us.

"Hey!" the gravelly voiced man croaked, "What in God's name are you doing?"

As he shuffled up closer, his features began to take on a familiar form. It was the poor old man everyone called Benny Borracho. Now things began to make sense to me.

Benny had been a fixture on the Santa Fe Plaza for many years. He could often be seen dozing on a bench, cradling a bottle wrapped in a brown paper bag, snoring loudly. Benny had a single-track mind. He was constantly pursuing spare change to secure his next bottle of Roma wine. He was a bit of an embarrassment, but he was harmless and tolerated. Actually, he did serve a purpose in his own roundabout way. He was held up as an example whenever kids failed to show proper motivation in doing their homework or completing their chores. Mamas all across Santa Fe exclaimed, "If you don't get on the ball and do as you're told, you'll end up like Benny Borracho."

Pepa anxiously hopped down from the tractor and stood next to me, facing the grizzled old man.

"Ah, hello Mr. Borracho," I mumbled. "How are you doing?"

The old man coughed hoarsely, spit on the ground, and peered down at us with beady, bloodshot eyes. "Don't tell me you kids are trying to run off with Zozobra? You could get in a heck of a lot of trouble for that."

I shot a look at Pepa. Thinking quickly, she took up the slack. "Oh, no sir. We were just moving him."

He looked at us and began to wheeze and shake. At first I was worried, but then I realized that Benny was laughing. He was laughing so hard that he had difficulty catching his breath. The tears rolled down his cheeks, and we stared at him open mouthed. After a few moments, he began to gain his composure.

"You think that I was born yesterday? I know what you're up to. You're stealing Zozobra because you're softhearted and don't want to see him burn. Isn't that right?"

Pepa and I looked at each other with a sinking feeling. We had been discovered, exposed. Our worst nightmare had come true. We stood silently, heads bowed, staring at the shoes of the old man.

"You know," continued Benny, "I never did like the way they burned up old Zozobra either. I wish I had the nerve to try something like you kids are doing. But if I ever got caught, they'd lock me up and throw away the key. No, I've seen enough of the inside of jail to last me a lifetime."

"By the way," he added, "you kids got any spare change?"

We stole a glance at each other and quickly dug through our pockets, coming up with sixty-eight cents in pennies, dimes, and nickels. We handed him the small mound of coins and peered at him expectantly.

He rubbed his bristly chin and said, "You kids listen up. I never saw nothing tonight, you understand? We never met each other on this bridge, okay? Nobody listens to an old wino like me anyway. You do what you have to do. I promise to Saint Christopher and Our Lady of Guadalupe that—what is that you called me? Oh, yeah—that Benny Borracho will never tell a soul what he has seen tonight. You kids get going and let me get some sleep. I have a feeling tomorrow's gonna be a pretty exciting day around here."

Pepa and I needed no prodding. We realized full well that we had dodged a bullet. Quickly, we jumped back onto the tractor and carefully dragged the patiently waiting Zozobra across the bridge.

We continued up the dirt road, and soon we were at the turn-off. We needed only one more piece of good luck to complete our mission. We had to remain undetected as we proceeded down the street and rode up to the national forest that was to be Zozobra's resting place.

A lucky star continued to follow us as we puffed along without interruption through the deserted street. The only sounds that broke the stillness of the night were the coughing tractor motor and the muffled scraping of Zozobra riding along on his bed of blankets.

We soon reached Artist Road and proceeded uphill toward the waiting mountains. In a few minutes, we'd traveled beyond the city proper and were climbing up a dark forest road to an isolated thicket of pine and aspen trees.

We stopped in a small clearing behind a tall clump of ponderosa pines. A little stream trickled nearby. Pepa and I were familiar with this spot. We had spent many warm summer afternoons here, away from parents, teachers, and the bustling humanity of the city. The remnants of an old clubhouse stood nestled against a large tree at the end of the site. We had started the structure the summer before, using sticks and twigs we had gathered nearby. However, halfway through the project our interest had waned. The crumbling abode stood as a monument to past dreams unfulfilled.

The liberated Zozobra rested in the middle of the clearing. When Pepa turned the tractor key off, the rattling motor came to a stop. The world was suddenly still and silent. We sat in the dark, listening to the quiet and reliving the past hour.

Soon my eyes adjusted to the dark. I focused on the huge figure that lay peacefully beside us. I could hardly believe that we had made this happen. The whole thing seemed like a dream. I felt relieved that it was over, and only then did I realize how tense the rescue had made me feel. I let out a sigh of relief and slapped Pepa's palm.

"We did it!" I whispered, breaking the silence.

"Yeah!" affirmed Pepa, in a voice filled with pride and satisfaction.

"You know," I admitted, "I was pretty nervous the whole time, especially when Benny came out of nowhere. But now I really feel like we did the right thing. I think that somewhere inside that big guy lying there is a big heart that's happy, because he knows he doesn't have to burn."

Pepa sat staring intently at Zozobra in the dark.

"I know what you mean. This whole thing was kinda scary, but we had to do it."

I nodded my head and watched her hop down from the tractor and begin untying Zozobra's arms and legs. I helped Pepa stuff the ropes and blankets back into the sacks. In a few minutes, we were ready to head back into town and the haven of our waiting beds.

The trip back to Victor's was uneventful as we rolled along in the cool night air. We guided the tractor back to the spot where it had been parked, put the ropes back in the shed, and returned the tractor key to its hiding place under the rock.

We were anxious to get home. We stashed the laundry bags full of blankets and supplies in an arroyo, under some weeds. Then we mounted our bikes and rode across the field and onto the dark streets. We were filled with a feeling of awe and life that is reserved only for heroes who have accomplished the impossible. Pepa and I exchanged farewells and slipped into our houses quietly. That night my sleep was deep and pure. I rested in the knowledge that I had scored a blow for justice and righted a major wrong.

The next morning, soon after the sun rose, my mother began to build a fire in the kitchen stove. She collected a handful of dry sticks from a basket near the kitchen door, tore a few strips from the previous day's newspaper, and started a small kindling fire in the center of the large cast-iron stove.

We were just sitting down to breakfast when someone knocked at the front door. My dad walked over and opened it. Alex Lujan, the sixteen-year-old paperboy, greeted him and handed him the morning edition of the *New Mexican*.

"Good morning, Alex. Anything new happening in the world today?"

"Boy, I'll say!" replied Alex. "You'll never believe what happened last night!" Alex's eyes were shining with excitement in the knowledge that he'd be the first source of the important information he was about to deliver to the Romero household.

"Well, Alex, what happened?" Dad prodded.

Alex exclaimed in a broken, adolescent voice, "Zozobra has escaped!"

"What?" laughed Dad.

"Zozobra escaped last night! Early this morning, when Mr. Gutiérrez, the milkman, was beginning his deliveries, he passed Fort Marcy Park and noticed that Zozobra was gone. He called the police and then the newspaper. There aren't many details in the morning edition, but we'll have more in the afternoon edition."

My dad whistled and shook his head. "This is one of the strangest things I've ever heard. Thanks for the paper, Alex." He walked back to the table, still shaking his head in disbelief. "Did you guys hear that?"

"Wow!" yelped little Angelo. "Zozobra got away! Papa, did he come alive and sneak away last night?"

"No, I don't think so."

"Still, this is very strange," my mom commented. "What do you think is going on, Gilbert?"

Dad peered out the window for a few moments, smoothing his mustache with his fingers. "It might be some sort of prank. Maybe some high school kids, some kind of initiation. Or maybe it could be some sort of publicity stunt cooked up by the Fiesta Council."

"All I know," he added, as he reached over and rubbed the top of Angelo's head, "is that old Zozobra did not get up and walk away by himself."

During the conversation, I sat quietly, staring at my hot bowl of atole. The reality of our deed was beginning to sink in. Thoughts were spinning inside my head so fast that I couldn't grab hold of one long enough to concentrate. The night before seemed like a dream or a story I had read about, something someone else had done. I couldn't believe there was such a fuss about it. The newspaper and the police investigating? I sat in a trance, half-listening.

My mom put her hand on my forehead and looked into my eyes with a worried expression. "Elvis," she said, "do you feel alright? You're so quiet this morning. You don't look yourself. You hardly touched your breakfast."

I smiled weakly. "No, I'm okay, really Mama. I'm just a little sleepy, I'm not very hungry."

She straightened her flower-print apron and said, "You're just overtired Elvis. You never slow down; you're always on the go." I nodded and began to head for the door.

She added, "Have a good day and work hard in school, *hijo*, and don't be so gloomy. You're beginning to look a little like Zozobra yourself!"

I forced a smile, waved good-bye, and walked outside toward my waiting bike. Riding in the cool morning air helped me feel a little better. I was glad to be out of the house and away from the inquiring glances of my mama. She could see through me in an instant.

I turned my bike onto East Alameda Street and rode toward Cristo Rey School. I rode through the entrance gate and parked next to several other bikes near the blue door of my classroom. I walked inside and took my seat in the second row. I shot a glance toward Pepa, who sat a row in front of me. Our eyes locked in secret acknowledgment.

We were still adjusting to the demands of normal life. I opened my math book and stared at the pages without focusing. Sister Angela led the class in the Lord's Prayer, and another school day began.

All through the morning I felt detached from the proceedings. Sister Angela's voice seemed distant like in a canyon. I kept thinking about what the paperboy had said. At last the lunch bell rang, and we were dismissed.

I waited by the door for Pepa, and we headed for the cafeteria. I related the paperboy's comments to Pepa as we ate lunch. We sat at an isolated table in a corner and conversed in low voices.

"Everybody in town is talking about it, Elvis. Early this morning, my *abuela* called my mama just to tell her about Zozobra."

I shook my head and looked across the gym at all the children eating. They were laughing and talking in lighthearted voices. I felt so much older. I wished I could be like they were, innocent and without care.

Pepa continued, "My mama said that without Zozobra, Fiesta just wouldn't be the same this year. She said that all the bad luck and gloom would stay with us if Zozobra didn't burn. I wanted to tell her that it wasn't Zozobra's fault and it wasn't fair to blame him for everything that went wrong, but I just kept quiet and left for school."

"Yeah, same here," I replied.

The bell rang, signaling the end of our lunch period, and we walked back to class. The afternoon went along much like the morning. I tried to concentrate on my work, but my mind was far away. When Sister Angela dismissed us at 3:00 p.m., I was desperate to escape and hop on my bike.

Pepa and I rode in silence, lost in our thoughts. I felt confused and worried. I hoped we had done the right thing. What else could we have done? As we headed home, past St. Francis Cathedral, I slowed down and stopped in front of the church.

"What's up?" shouted Pepa.

"I think I'll sit in the church for a little while."

Although this was highly unusual behavior, Pepa nodded her head in agreement. Given our present situation, she understood my desire to seek guidance and refuge.

We parked our bikes against a black iron railing that separated church property from a small grassy park. We walked up to the massive wooden doors of the great cathedral and entered the sanctuary. The air inside was sweet with the smell of incense and flowers.

Pepa and I dipped our fingers in a small bowl of holy water sitting on a table to our right. We made the sign of the cross and reverently stepped forward into the church. We both genuflected and knelt down at a wooden pew in the back, facing the altar.

The imposing cathedral that Sister Angela had told us about in our history lessons was built by Archbishop Lamy in 1886. It was an overwhelming structure. The afternoon light streamed through the stained-glass windows depicting various saints and stations of the cross. The high ceilings and a finely carved crucifix, which dominated the altar, gave the church an unearthly atmosphere.

We prayed in silence, our heads bowed and hands clasped. After a few minutes of meditation, I raised my head and noticed a small line of people standing by the confessional at the front of the church.

As a boy, I was taught that confession was an important aspect in leading a good, Catholic life. The act of confession consisted of entering a small wood-paneled booth, separated by a cloth-screened window from another booth, in which a priest sat. The screen did not allow the priest or the confessor to see each other, but they could speak through the opening.

The confessor listed all the sins he had committed since his last confession had taken place. Based on the nature and frequency of sins, the priest recommended an appropriate penance, usually in the form of prayers to be recited. The confession also allowed the priest to give advice and counsel. After the sinner had completed his penance, he received a Holy Communion wafer at Mass the following Sunday. As a result of these efforts, in the eyes of the church and God, all his sins were forgiven and he could begin life anew.

I felt compelled to take confession and relieve my troubled soul. I rose from the pew and walked toward the line of Catholic faithful. I turned and glanced at Pepa, who shook her head, indicating that she wished to stay behind.

After a brief pause, I opened the polished wooden door and entered the dark booth. I sat in silence until the priest cleared his throat, indicating that I could begin.

I recited the traditional beginning to confession that I had been taught in catechism class. "Bless me, Father, for I have sinned. My last confession was three weeks ago. I am sorry for these sins and the sins of my whole life."

After a short pause, I began to recount my fantastic adventure to the priest behind the screen. I retraced my actions, thoughts, and feelings, as he sat listening silently. As I told my story, the pit in my stomach began to dissipate, and I felt a sense of relief settling over me. The long arms of the church embraced me. I felt secure within their grasp. When I completed my confession, I sat quietly, waiting for advice and spiritual direction.

The priest paused for a few moments and began to speak. "My son," he began in a compassionate voice, "my impression is that you are a boy with a good heart who is trying his best to do what is just. However, I wonder if you have really thought about all the consequences of your actions. Do you understand what I'm saying?"

"Yes, Father," I whispered solemnly.

The priest continued, "In his own special way, Zozobra has a mission to fulfill. I understand how you and probably many other children feel about Zozobra. It is sad to watch him burn at Fiesta. But have you considered that perhaps Zozobra has his own fate? Could you deny him the purpose of his existence? This has been a difficult year for many people in Santa Fe. The passing of their troubles symbolized in the burning of Zozobra could mean a great deal to them."

As I sat listening to his words, I began to see Zozobra in a different light. I started thinking that maybe Zozobra would do more good washing away the sorrows of the past year than lying in the woods, slowly falling apart. Still, one more detail troubled me.

"Father?" I asked cautiously.

"Yes, son?"

"I understand everything that you've told me. I think you're right about Zozobra and everything, but what should I do now? I mean, should I tell my parents or the police? I don't know what to do."

The priest pondered this point for a few moments and replied, "Let me take care of letting the proper people know where Zozobra is. That is, if I have your permission. Remember, everything we talk about in confession is confidential."

"Yes, Father. You have my permission."

"Very well then. In this case, I believe it is not necessary to confess your actions to anyone but God. You acted with a pure heart. After all, that is what really matters. As long as they get Zozobra back, I don't think it's so important for them to know who took him in the first place."

"Thank you, Father," I whispered.

"Your penance is to recite the Lord's Prayer ten times and also to pray ten Hail Mary's every night before bed for the next ten days. Peace be with you my son."

"And with you Father," I answered.

I stood up and left the confessional. Walking toward the pew at the back of the church where Pepa sat, I felt lighter, like a great weight had been lifted from me. Pepa rose when I approached. We knelt in front of the altar and left the church.

We walked to a stone bench in the nearby park. As we sat in the shade of a fat cottonwood tree, I recounted my discussion with the priest. Pepa sat silently and gazed at the lilac bushes lining the path.

I waited for her response nervously, but for a long time she showed no reaction. At last she turned her eyes to me. I could see they were filled with tears. She choked back a sob and said, "How could you give Zozobra away? I thought I could trust you, Elvis. Now look what you've done."

Her words stung me like cactus needles. I felt a hot flash of emotion travel up into my head. Tears started to rise in my eyes as well, and everything was suddenly blurry.

"Didn't you hear what the priest said, Pepa? What was I supposed to do? Wouldn't you have done the same thing? Think about it. What would Fiesta be like if we kept Zozobra a secret? So many people are counting on him to burn, so that things will go better for everybody. Maybe it was selfish of us to only think about what we felt like. You know what I mean? Besides, Zozobra isn't like a real person. He's just a bunch of stuffed rags."

As soon as I said this, I knew I had gone too far. Pepa lifted her head, glared at me, and spit on the ground.

"Fine, Elvis! Now you decide Zozobra isn't worth it! Why didn't you think about all this before? It could have saved both of us a lot of trouble. Sometimes I don't understand you, Elvis. Sometimes I don't understand you."

Pepa covered her eyes with her hands and began to weep.

She sobbed, "I'm all confused."

My blood began to cool down. I walked over to Pepa and put my hand on her shoulder.

"Come on. I don't wanna fight about it. We did what we thought was right. It's just that now I'm not so sure we were thinking straight. Let's get going."

Pepa rubbed her eyes and sighed deeply. She suddenly stood up and rubbed the top of my head vigorously and laughed as she shouted, "Tonto!"

I saw the heaviness leave her body, and the old Pepa was back again. My heart swelled with love and friendship for my faithful amiga.

We decided it was our duty to visit Zozobra one last time before we headed home. We rode up Washington Avenue, turned on Artist Road, and soon reached the secret clearing that shielded Zozobra. The giant lay still, staring into the sky as if he had not noticed our arrival. We stood at his feet, gazing at his frozen face.

"I don't think he looks too happy here," I said. "The priest was right. Zozobra needs to fulfill his destiny."

Pepa nodded in agreement and added, "You know, I'm still gonna miss him."

I felt a sense of sadness mingled with the relief I had felt after confession. There was still a part of me that felt sorry for Zozobra. We stood silently and said our personal good-byes to him.

Pepa broke the silence and in a business-like voice exclaimed, "I guess we'd better be getting back home." I agreed, and we rode off without a backward glance, leaving Zozobra to his fate.

A few minutes later we parted company. I rode up to my little adobe house. My mom was in the yard pulling weeds from her small garden of tomatoes and cucumbers. She stood up, wiped the dirt off her hands, and hugged me as I walked into the yard.

Cómo estas, mi hijo? she said. "Lately, you've been looking like you're carrying the whole world on your shoulders. Go inside and rest. I made you some fresh tortillas with butter and honey." As I stepped toward the house, she added, "Don't worry so much, Elvis. Everything will turn out all right if you have a good heart and try to do the right thing."

"I'm trying, Mama," I said as I walked through the front door. "I'm trying."

WELL, THAT IS MY STORY, dear readers. I hope you found it entertaining, if nothing else. Some of you may find our adventure a bit hard to believe, but strange things happen when determined children set their minds to something. Pepa and I both have children of our own now, and every year our families get together during Fiesta. We reminisce about our escapade, but our children just roll their eyes and complain, "Not that story again!" Viva la Fiesta!

Fiesta de Santa Fe: A History

HE CITIZENS OF SANTA FE have been celebrating the annual Fiesta for nearly three centuries, making it the oldest community celebration in the United States. Multiple generations of Santa Feans have witnessed and participated in the festivities. Certainly, it is a commemoration of historical and religious events, but it is more than that. It is also a celebration of culture.

A diversity of cultures has played a major part in making the Santa Fe Fiesta what it is today. More specifically, it is a celebration of people, past and present, who have struggled to survive and thrive in this high-desert environment.

The Fiesta de Santa Fe has always had an influential role in defining the city's self-identity. It has been a barometer reflecting community, social, and political attitudes. Santa Fe and the Fiesta are intimately linked, and the Fiesta tells the story of Santa Fe's evolution.

From its founding, Santa Fe had the audacity to invent its own identity. Indeed, it had to. As a remote northern outpost of the Spanish and Mexican governments in Mexico City, Santa Fe developed in relative isolation.

IN THE 1920S a free-thinking art colony that was developing in Santa Fe expressed its displeasure with the staged Fiesta that was organized by the Museum of New Mexico by creating alternative Fiesta activities called "El Pasa-tiempo." One of these new events was a "Hysterical Parade" that emphasized fun and irreverence. Shown here is the "Toonerville Trolley" Fiesta float occupied by jovial parade participants. Photo by T. Harmon Parkhurst, courtesy Palace of the Governors Photo Archives (NMHM/DCA), 117681.

The "City Different" has always prided itself on its diversity and its acceptance of those with new ideas and atypical points of view. This open, liberal atmosphere has had an appeal to many. Santa Fe is unique in its cultural mix and openness to various social and religious beliefs. It is known widely as a New Age mecca. One can find Catholic churches on Indian pueblos and non-Native seekers embracing Native American religious values. Temples and worshippers of faiths spanning the entire planet are part of the city's spiritual climate.

This tolerant thinking is not new. The seeds were cultivated in the late 1800s and early 1900s, when writers, artists, and other Americans seeking an alternative lifestyle ventured west and settled side by side with the indigenous Indian and Spanish colonial cultures. People learned to live together in this special place. The Santa Fe Fiesta evolved as a perfect example of this hybrid, as Spanish religious activities were successfully balanced with Anglo-American contributions such as Zozobra, the Historical/Hysterical Parade, and the Fiesta Melodrama.

Santa Fe has lived easily with contradiction and paradox. Social lines are easily blurred, as evidenced by rich folks driving beat-up pickups; ethnically mixed couples; and locals, tourists, and the homeless sharing the Plaza harmoniously.

THIS DE VARGAS PAGEANT procession paraded down Palace Avenue in 1911. A concern for historical accuracy was not always present, particularly in regard to Pueblo Indian dress. Stereotypical images of Indians in Plains-style headdress and attire were commonly used to portray Pueblo Indians. Photo courtesy Palace of the Governors Photo Archives (NMHM/DCA), 158206.

Fiesta de Santa Fe Timeline

La Conquistadora

The story of the Santa Fe Fiesta begins in 1625 with a Marion bulto figure carved out of willow and olive wood that stood twenty-eight inches high. A Franciscan priest, Fray Alonzo de Benavidez, brought this representation of the Blessed Virgin Mary to Santa Fe from Mexico City to provide inspiration for the Spanish colonists.

She was originally named Our Lady of Assumption. Sometime between 1630 and 1656 she was renamed Our Lady of the Rosary and a confraternity, Confradia de Rosario, was formed in her honor. Her final name change occurred sometime before 1680, when she was given the title Nuestra Señora de la Conquistadora. Historian Thomas Chavez points out that the term conquistadora meant "to win one's heart and affection" at that time. Religion was very important, and La Conquistadora was an important icon of hope and devotion.

The Pueblo Revolt and the Spanish Reconquest

The Pueblo Revolt in 1680 drove the Spaniards out of Santa Fe. On August 11, 1680, under the leadership of a Tewa warrior named Popé, the Pueblo Revolt began. The Spanish retreated from Santa Fe and traveled three hundred miles south to El Paso del Norte, near present-day Ciudad Juarez, Mexico. Legend has it that La Conquistadora was rescued from a burning church and accompanied the fleeing Spaniards.

In 1692 the king of Spain appointed Don Diego de Vargas as the new captain-general and governor of New Mexico. He met with Indian leaders to ask that the Spanish settlers be allowed to return peacefully. His plan was to announce his arrival and to ask the Pueblo Indians to return to Spanish rule and the Catholic

Church. Vargas visited all twenty-three pueblos, negotiating with each without firing a single shot or losing a soldier. He then went back to El Paso del Norte to plan the larger resettlement.

Vargas was convinced that his first mission had been successful, and he returned in 1693 with eighteen friars, seventy families, and thousands of horses, mules, and livestock. He came back to find that the Pueblo Indians had not vacated Santa Fe as he had expected and were hesitant to return to Spanish rule. The settlers spent much of December in a bitterly cold camp north of Santa Fe, suffering from exposure. On December 28, 1693, Vargas abandoned the plan for a peaceful return and laid siege to Santa Fe.

The Connection between Vargas and La Conquistadora

Vargas wrote that he wished to return to Santa Fe to establish La Conquistadora's reign over the kingdom of New Mexico. He prayed for her intervention to make the reconquest end successfully.

After the Spanish returned in 1693, Vargas had La Conquistadora temporarily enshrined in a chapel in Casas Reales, while a church was built in her honor. Vargas died in 1704, and the church he envisioned was not completed until 1714.

In 1712, eight years after Vargas's death, a group of Spanish colonists led by Juan Paz Hurtado (Vargas's former lieutenant governor) met to observe his memory. They drafted a proclamation to commemorate the reconquest and Vargas's memory with an annual fiesta. The year 1712 is cited as the historical beginning of the Santa Fe Fiesta.

The Early Santa Fe Fiesta

Fiesta observances throughout the 1700s and 1800s were not well documented. However, it is known that they were primarily religious in nature, with the Corpus Christi and La Conquistadora

LA CONQUISTADORA

accompanied Vargas's struggle to recapture Santa Fe. Photo by Tyler Dingee, courtesy Palace of the Governors Photo Archives (NMHM/DCA), 73832.

ELEGANTLY COSTUMED SPANISH DANCERS,

ca 1940s–1950s, add color and style to the Fiesta de Santa Fe. Traditional New Mexican dances, such as polkas, waltzes, and rancheras, were among the cultural offerings of Fiesta. New Mexico Magazine Collection, courtesy Palace of the Governors Photo Archives (NMHM/DCA).

DE VARGAS PAGEANT

procession down Lincoln Avenue in 1911. As Santa Fe and the rest of New Mexico approached statehood, the city embraced military marching bands and automobiles as proof New Mexico was American enough to become part of the United States. Photo by Jesse Nusbaum, courtesy Palace of the Governors Photo Archives (NMHM/DCA), 118260.

DE VARGAS PAGEANT
in the courtyard of the Palace
of the Governors in 1919. The
Fiesta increasingly was organized
and staged by the Museum of
New Mexico and the School of
American Research after 1919.
This would lead to increasing
disenchantment by local residents.
Photo by Jesse Nusbaum, courtesy
Palace of the Governors Photo
Archives (NMHM/DCA), 118452.

processions being the main points of focus. Early Fiesta processions included the use of evergreens to line the procession routes.

In 1807 Rosario Chapel was built on the spot where La Conquistadora was believed to have sat during Vargas's entrada into Santa Fe in 1693. This has been an important landmark for La Conquistadora processions ever since.

Santa Fe became a Mexican territory in 1821 following the Mexican Revolution, but this did not affect local devotion for La Conquistadora or the observance of the Fiesta. The residents of Santa Fe were far removed from the upheaval of the Mexican war.

However, other changes resulting from the Mexican Revolution would eventually profoundly influence Santa Fe and the Fiesta. A policy that had a far-reaching impact on Santa Fe was the openness of the new Mexican government to trade with the United States. The Santa Fe Trail between Santa Fe and Independence, Missouri, was established in 1821. Santa Fe became a trading center when the Santa Fe Trail connected with the Chihuahua Trail (Camino Real) and the Old Spanish Trail.

In 1846 three hundred U.S. troops led by Gen. Stephen Watts Kearny and supported by one thousand mounted volunteers left Independence, Missouri, and marched 856 miles to Santa Fe to occupy the city. Santa Fe was in no position to mount much of a defense. Lack of support from the central government in Mexico had left the local militia depleted. Knowing they were no match for the advancing U.S. forces, Governor Manuel Armijo and many others decided to flee. On August 18, 1846, Kearny marched into Santa Fe unopposed. Not a drop of blood was spilled in the occupation.

The designation of New Mexico as a U.S. territory in 1850 opened the gates to a steady stream of Americans from the East. The occupation and designation as a U.S. territory also permanently transformed Santa Fe and the Fiesta.

Perhaps the event that did the most to change the nature of the territory was the coming of the railroad in 1880. New people arrived by the thousands. Between 1880 and 1900, the Anglo-American population of New Mexico quadrupled.

Anglo-American Influence on the Fiesta

As more Anglo-Americans migrated to Santa Fe, the Fiesta was no longer the only major festival in town. The Fourth of July held equal importance. In 1883 the two events were merged and became a prototype of future Fiestas.

The 1883 Fiesta/Tertio-Millennial Exposition was a major undertaking. It was a celebration to commemorate the 333rd anniversary of the founding of Santa Fe. In fact, the year 1550 had no significance in Santa Fe history, but that didn't matter. The exposition's purpose was to promote Santa Fe as an emerging center of business and tourism.

The Fiesta radically shifted in nature that year. It featured businessmen and farmers displaying their goods, as well as horse races, parades, music, and dancing. The three-day affair featured Indian Day the first day, the reenactment of the Vargas entrada on the second day, and Anglo-American culture on the final day.

That year marked the transformation of the Fiesta from a mainly religious festival into more of a civic celebration. The revised Fiesta/Fourth of July celebration continued to thrive from 1883 up until New Mexico statehood in 1912.

The new diversity contained in the revised Fiesta was exemplified by a local gentleman named George Washington Armijo. He played the role of Don Diego de Vargas in 1911. He had been a Rough Rider with Teddy Roosevelt during the Spanish American War. Also in 1911, in another tip of the hat to diversity, both the Mexican and U.S. national anthems were played during Fiesta.

The year 1912 marked a grand Fiesta celebrating New Mexico statehood. Participants included the Chamber of Commerce, the Alianza Hispano-Americana, and the Museum of New Mexico.

INDIAN DANCES were a prominent part of the 1919 Fiesta program, as with this Eagle Dance performed by dancers from San Ildefonso Pueblo in the courtyard of the Palace of the Governors. Photo by Wesley Bradfield, courtesy Palace of the Governors Photo Archives (NMHM/DCA), 52430.

THE PROMINENCE of American flags and soldiers in uniform in 1919 reveals the level of American patriotism felt by Santa Feans after statehood was granted. Photo by Wesley Bradfield, courtesy Palace of the Governors Photo Archives (NMHM/DCA), 52392.

The Fiesta after Statehood

Despite the enthusiasm of the 1912 Fiesta, the civic aspect of the celebration was dropped for the next six years and not revived until 1919. One major factor was World War I. Santa Fe was now a U.S. city and was preoccupied with other matters. It is important to note that even though the outward civic celebration did not take place, the Fiesta was still observed as a religious event during this period. It became much like earlier Fiesta celebrations that were almost exclusively devotional in nature. Thus the Santa Fe Fiesta can still claim to have been continuously observed for almost three hundred years without interruption.

The year 1919 represented another turning point for the Fiesta. The community celebration was revived and organized by the Museum of New Mexico and the School of American Research, made up of mostly eastern-educated non-locals. Hispanic participation dropped sharply. The Fiesta was being redefined by outsiders, and its cultural and religious identity was being lost in the eyes of the local population. Even though George Washington Armijo agreed once again to play the role of Don Diego de Vargas, most of those in his *cuadrilla*, or retinue, were non-Hispanics.

The Santa Fe Art Colony and the Fiesta

The local Hispanic population found unusual allies who shared their displeasure with what the Santa Fe Fiesta had become. A group of free-thinking, creatively oriented individuals were drawn to Santa Fe in the early 1920s in search of a more meaningful lifestyle. They were fleeing the industrial culture of the eastern United States. Many of these disaffected newcomers were artists, writers, and photographers.

The Museum of New Mexico, in an attempt to make the Fiesta financially self-sustaining, had fenced off certain Fiesta activities and priced out many people, much to the consternation of local Hispanos and art colony activists. In response, to rival the organized Fiesta, these groups began a program of free Fiesta activities under the name of El Pasatiempo. These new activities included a Hysterical Parade featuring exaggerated dress, community street singing and dancing, a children's animal parade, and of course Zozobra.

Zozobra and Other 1920s Fiesta Innovations

In 1924 artist Will Shuster constructed a puppet based on an effigy of Judas that he had seen burned in a ritual in Mexico. He burned the puppet in his backyard for a few friends. The next year, with the help of E. Dana Johnson, the editor of the *Santa Fe New Mexican*, he increased the puppet's size to eighteen feet and gave it the name Zozobra, which roughly translates to "gloomy or anguished one." In 1926 the first public burning of Shuster's Zozobra took place, and a Fiesta tradition was born. In following years, the burning came to signify the beginning of the Fiesta.

In 1927 a Fiesta Queen was added to complement the Don Diego de Vargas role. The 1920s also saw renewed religious activities, as Hispanic participation increased. In 1920 the Fiesta was highlighted by the dedication of the Cross of the Martyrs, a monument to the twenty-one priests killed during the 1680 Pueblo Revolt. In 1925 a Candlelight Procession to the Cross of the Martyrs was added as an annual Fiesta event.

By the late 1920s, the local community had taken on more ownership, and many of the diverse El Pasatiempo influences became a permanent part of the traditional Fiesta.

The Contemporary Fiesta

The 1950s saw Santa Fe's continued growth and an obsession with tourism after World War II. Art came to be a vital industry in the city, and art galleries sprung up around the Plaza and along Canyon Road. The Santa Fe Opera opened in 1957, drawing performers and visitors from around the world. In the 1960s, tourism and government were the primary employers in Santa Fe.

In 1964 the Archdiocese of Santa Fe withdrew its support of the Fiesta because of a perception that the event had become too commercialized and had lost its religious focus. However, church support was reinstated in 1966 after the Fiesta Council promised to place more emphasis on religious aspects.

The Fiesta began to attract large numbers of visitors from outside Santa Fe in the 1960s, partly because the celebration was held during the Labor Day weekend. Most visitors had little knowledge of the history and customs of the Fiesta. This led to local dissatisfaction with the direction of the Fiesta.

The definitive event that led to a shift away from the Labor Day Fiesta occurred in 1971. Civil disobedience during the Fiesta led to widespread vandalism in the downtown area and confrontations with the police. About one hundred National Guard reserves were called to the Plaza to restore order. This incident was referred to as the Fiesta Riots by locals. It led to an effort to make the Fiesta smaller and more local.

The Kidnapping of La Conquistadora

Another event that shook the foundations of the Fiesta occurred on March 19, 1973, when La Conquistadora was kidnapped. It was speculated that the perpetrators hid in the choir loft at St. Francis Cathedral and carried her out of the building without detection. Church, media, and public officials raised their voices in outrage, and local groups raised reward money. On March 25, the mayor's office declared a day of mourning. Bells tolled in the city, and church leaders asked for prayers for La Conquistadora's safe return.

Three weeks later, a ransom note demanding $150,000 was received. On April 15, after a massive search by state and local police, she was found in an abandoned Valencia County mine in the foothills of the Manzano Mountains. Two local teenage boys were arrested after their failed extortion attempt. La Conquistadora's return was marked by a solemn procession. The mayor called the homecoming "a most memorable day in the history of Santa Fe."

Gathering Up Again: The Santa Fe Fiesta

A 1992 video documentary examined the Santa Fe Fiesta with a critical eye and presented a Pueblo Indian perspective. The documentary, *Gathering Up Again: The Santa Fe Fiesta*, generated debate among local leaders. It was also a catalyst for change. The following year, Archbishop Robert Sanchez gave La Conquistadora an additional name, Señora de la Paz, or Our Lady of Peace. A Mass of Reconciliation was added to the Fiesta. A move to more cultural sensitivity toward Pueblo people during the Fiesta was encouraged.

The Santa Fe Tourist Boom

In the early 1980s, a tourism explosion transformed Santa Fe into an international travel destination. Various media sources announced to the world that Santa Fe was the "in place" to be. The media attention led to a swelling of tourism and an influx of wealthy new residents in the 1980s and 1990s. Ritzy shops sprang up everywhere, while home and land prices in Santa Fe climbed upward.

In 1990, for the first time in the city's history, the Anglo population surpassed that of Hispanic residents. Santa Fe was fast becoming a place that was too expensive for local people to live in. In the 1990s, the city's Office of Community Development estimated that Santa Fe's middle class was shrinking at the rate of two percent per year.

These changes have led to a sense of loss for many Santa Feans. Santa Fe in the twenty-first century is a community at the crossroads, attempting to create a future that can accommodate change and also preserve the culture and integrity of its past.

FIESTA, San Francisco Street, 1932. Photo by T. Harmon Parkhurst, courtesy Palace of the Governors Photo Archives (NMHM/DCA), 68822.

SANTA FE FLOAT IN THE
1950 ROSE PARADE, Pasa-
dena, California. Courtesy Palace
of the Governors Photo Archives
(NMHM/DCA), 049923.

Santa Fe has gone through a number of dramatic changes in recent years. The local economy and lifestyle have been strongly affected by these social transformations. Santa Fe's population continues to grow. The city's population increased from about twenty thousand in 1945 to forty thousand in 1970 to sixty-two thousand in 2000. In 2010 the population was close to seventy-five thousand. Long-term issues such as adequate water resources and quality of life are major concerns.

The Cultural Significance of the Fiesta de Santa Fe

The one constant that Santa Fe has retained is its fervent celebration of the Fiesta, which brings city residents together and for many evokes a spirit of nostalgia and historical/cultural reverence.

The Santa Fe Fiesta remains a touchstone of identity for many Santa Feans, regardless of ethnicity, culture, or religious background. It is a statement proclaiming: "This is my town, and I am part of a unique community." Many historic traditions and rituals remain a vital part of the celebration, providing a continuity of past and present.

The Fiesta de Santa Fe is as vital and vibrant today as ever. There will always be concerns regarding perceived commercialism, safety issues, and differences of opinion about where resources and emphasis should be placed, but the Fiesta will continue to be observed and cherished as long as Santa Fe remains a vibrant community.

ZOZOBRA, ca. 1940s–1950s. New Mexico Magazine Collection, courtesy Palace of the Governors Photo Archives (NMHM/DCA).

Project editor: Mary Wachs
Art and production direction: David Skolkin
Design: Jason Valdez
Manufactured in China
10 9 8 7 6 5 4 3 2 1

Museum of New Mexico Press
Post Office Box 2087
Santa Fe, New Mexico 87504
www.mnmpress.org